HERO
6

HIRO
TO THE
RESCUE!

randomhousekids.com

ISBN 978-0-7364-3243-6 (trade) — ISBN 978-0-7364-8154-0 (lib. bdg.)

Printed in the United States of America
10 9 8 7 6 5 4 3 2 1

HIRO
TO THE
RESCUE!

By Victoria Saxon

Illustrated by
the Disney Storybook Art Team

Random House New York

Chapter 1

A large crowd stood in an alley in the city of San Fransokyo. They watched as two robots got ready to fight.

Fourteen-year-old Hiro Hamada waited. One of the robots was his, and it would be fighting Mr. Yama's robot. Mr. Yama's robot was the current champion.

"Two bots enter. One bot leaves," the referee said, looking from one to the other. "Fighters ready? Fight!"

It was over in seconds. One robot was fast and broke the other robot into pieces. The crowd was silent. Hiro's robot had won!

Mr. Yama was angry. "No one can beat Little Yama!" he shouted. "You cheated, and I want to know how!"

Mr. Yama grew angrier. His men closed in on Hiro.

Just then, Hiro's eighteen-year-old brother, Tadashi, drove up on his motor scooter.

"Get on!" Tadashi shouted. Hiro jumped on the scooter, and they raced through the streets. Mr. Yama's men chased them. They drove until they were safe. Tadashi took them to the campus of San Fransokyo Institute of Technology, known as SFIT, where he was a student.

"What are we doing at your nerd school?" Hiro asked.

Tadashi used his ID to get into the robotics lab. "Relax, you big baby," he said. "We'll be in and out. Anyway, you've never seen my lab."

Hiro rolled his eyes as he followed his brother down the hallway. "Oh, great, I get to see your lab."

"Heads up!" A blur on a bike zoomed past them in the hallway before

stopping right in front of the two brothers.

Hiro's eyes widened when he saw the mag-lev wheels.

"Whoa!"

The bike rider removed her helmet and snapped her gum. "Who are you?"

"Um, I'm . . . Tadashi's brother . . . ," Hiro stammered.

Tadashi smiled and introduced his kid brother to his friend. "Go Go, this is Hiro."

Go Go Tomago was an industrial designer who loved to ride fast.

Tadashi led Hiro into the lab and introduced the rest of his friends.

Wasabi was a physics student who loved organization. He showed Hiro his invention—an optic laser system that could cut items into wafer-thin slices.

Honey Lemon was a chemistry genius and the happiest person on earth. "Oh my gosh, hi!" she said to Hiro. "Perfect timing. You are going to love this!"

After selecting a few chemicals, Honey whipped up a pink goo. She put the mixture on top of a metal sphere. When she touched the metal with one finger, the metal turned into dust.

Then there was Fred. He was the school mascot, even though he wasn't a student, and he didn't invent things. He just liked hanging out with the rest of the group.

Hiro saw that Tadashi had walked to the other side of the lab. He joined his brother. "So, what have you been working on?"

Tadashi put a piece of duct tape on Hiro's arm. Then he ripped it off. "Oww!" Hiro exclaimed.

From a suitcase at Tadashi's feet, a white robot emerged and instantly filled with air.

"Hello. I am Baymax, your personal health-care companion," the friendly, huggable bot said.

"A nurse robot?" Hiro asked Tadashi.

"I programmed him with more than ten thousand medical procedures," Tadashi explained. He showed Hiro a green chip in Baymax's chest. "This chip is home to the caregiving matrix that makes Baymax . . . Baymax!"

Baymax scanned Hiro's injury and sprayed it with medicine.

Tadashi said Baymax could also lift

heavy weights. "He's going to help a lot of people."

"I cannot deactivate until you say that you are satisfied with my care," Baymax said.

"Well, then: I am satisfied with my care," Hiro said. At Hiro's statement, Baymax deflated and folded himself back into his suitcase.

The brothers were surprised to hear another voice. Professor Robert Callaghan, who taught robotics, was standing behind them. Tadashi was excited to introduce him to Hiro.

The professor stared at the fighting bot in Hiro's hands. "May I?" he asked.

"Uh, sure," Hiro said, reluctantly handing it to the professor.

Callaghan asked where Hiro had

learned to make it.

"Taught myself," Hiro said.

"Have you thought of applying here?" Callaghan asked.

"Actually, sir, my brother's pretty serious about his career in bot-fighting," Tadashi said, giving the professor a wink.

Callaghan stared at Hiro. "I can see why. With your bot, winning must come easy."

"Yeah, I guess," Hiro said.

"Well, if you like things easy, then my program isn't for you," Callaghan said. "My students go on to shape the future."

For once, Hiro didn't know how to respond.

Hiro and Tadashi said goodbye and

then went outside. Hiro stared at his brother. He was no longer thinking about bot fighting. "If I don't go to this nerd school, I'm gonna lose my mind!"

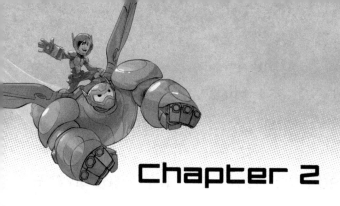

Chapter 2

SFIT sponsored an annual Tech Showcase. Anyone could enter, and the kids with the best tech won admission to the school!

"Come up with something that blows Callaghan away, you're in!" Tadashi told his brother.

Hiro got to work. In a makeshift lab in his aunt Cass's garage, he worked night and day. When it was time for the showcase, Hiro was ready.

Hiro, Tadashi, and their friends arrived at the showcase early. The building was packed. Hiro moved quickly through the crowd.

"I really want to go here," Hiro told Tadashi. He didn't want to blow his chance to get into SFIT.

"Just take a deep breath," Tadashi said. "You got this."

When it was time, Hiro walked onto the stage. He began to speak, and the microphone squealed with feedback. He nervously put on an electronic headband. Then he opened one of his hands. In it was a small black piece of metal.

"This is a microbot," Hiro said. But the crowd wasn't paying attention.

Offstage, Tadashi gave his brother a thumbs-up. He knew Hiro could blow the crowd away and win them over.

"It doesn't look like much," Hiro said, "but when it links up with the rest of its pals . . ."

Suddenly, the whole room buzzed with microbots. They moved through the crowd like a swarm of insects and gathered onstage. Now people were paying attention!

"The microbots are controlled by this neural transmitter." Hiro pointed to his headband. "I think what I want them to do, and they do it."

The microbots joined together and formed the shape of a hand.

Hiro used his microbots to show that one person could move big objects.

Eventually, people using the microbots would be able to save time and money. They could even save lives by sending bots into dangerous situations instead of humans.

The crowd roared with approval. They loved Hiro's bots!

One man, Alistair Krei, was particularly impressed. He was the owner of a large tech company, and he wanted to talk to Hiro.

When Hiro exited the stage, Krei took one of Hiro's microbots and held it in his hand. "With some development, these could be revolutionary," he said. "You are about to become a very wealthy kid."

Hiro was surprised. *Krei wants to buy my microbots?*

Professor Callaghan walked over.

"This is your decision, Hiro, but you should know that Mr. Krei has cut corners and ignored sound science to get where he is."

Krei objected. "That's just not true—"

Callaghan cut him off. "I wouldn't trust him with your microbots . . . or anything else."

Hiro was quiet as he looked from one man to the other.

"I appreciate the offer, Mr. Krei," said Hiro. "But I'm sorry, they're not for sale."

Krei turned to walk away.

"Mr. Krei," Tadashi said, "that's my brother's."

Krei looked at his hand, still gripping the tiny robot. "Oh, right," he said, chuckling, and gave it back to Hiro.

When the showcase ended, the brothers got great news. Hiro's microbot had impressed the judges. He had won a spot at SFIT! They walked outside. They looked at the campus. Tadashi put his arm around Hiro.

"The Hamada brothers are going to do big things," Tadashi said.

"We're gonna change the world,

right?" Hiro added proudly.

Suddenly, the doors burst open and people ran from the showcase. Someone yelled, "Fire!"

"Hey, are you okay?" Tadashi asked a student running past.

"I'm fine. Callaghan's still in there!"

Tadashi moved toward the hall. Hiro grabbed his brother's shirt.

"Tadashi, no!" he shouted.

His brother looked at him. "Callaghan's in there. Someone has to help!"

Hiro let go. Then he watched Tadashi run inside the hall. There was a loud explosion.

"Tadashi!" Hiro screamed. But Tadashi didn't come back.

The next day, people began putting flowers on the steps leading to the robotics lab in honor of both Tadashi and Professor Callaghan.

Honey, Wasabi, Go Go, and Fred found Hiro. They hugged him. Nothing helped.

Tears ran down the boy's face. "Tadashi!" he cried.

Chapter 3

Rain hit the window of Hiro and Tadashi's room. It was quiet. Tadashi's baseball cap lay on his bed.

Hiro sat alone on his beanbag chair with his old battle bot in his hands.

Aunt Cass knocked on the door.

"Hey, sweetie!" she said. Aunt Cass tried to sound happy. She brought Hiro breakfast. She went to the window and raised the blinds. "You get any sleep?"

She looked at his plate of food from the night before. He hadn't eaten a thing. "The university called again," she added. "It's not too late to register."

"I'll think about it," Hiro said.

Aunt Cass quietly left. Hiro got up and closed the window blinds. School had started. But Hiro no longer cared.

Hiro headed toward his bed and dropped his battle bot on his toe. "Ow!"

Something moved near Tadashi's bed.

Baymax, Tadashi's robot, inflated to full size. He had been in the room since the showcase! Hiro's cry of pain had made him activate.

Hiro was so shocked to see him, he tripped.

"On a scale of one to ten, how would

you rate your pain?" Baymax asked.

"Zero," Hiro answered, wishing Baymax would return to his charging station.

Baymax scanned Hiro. "No injuries," he reported. "However, your hormone and neurotransmitter levels indicate that you are experiencing mood swings; common in adolescence. Diagnosis: puberty."

"Whoa! What?" Hiro said. "Okay, time to shrink now!" He pushed the robot toward his charging station.

Baymax continued. "You should experience an increase in body hair—"

"Thank you!" Hiro shouted. He did not want to hear about body hair!

Hiro tripped and fell. As he lay on the floor, he heard a noise coming from a hoodie peeking out from under his bed.

A microbot was in one of the pockets! It was the one that Alistair Krei had handed back to him. It had survived the fire at the showcase because Hiro had taken it home.

The microbot buzzed! Hiro placed it in a petri dish. *It's rattling against the glass like it wants to join the other microbots,* Hiro thought. *But the others were destroyed in the fire!*

"Dumb thing's broken!" he said.

Baymax was interested in the microbot. "Your tiny robot is trying to go somewhere," he said.

Hiro sat down at his desk and began working on his fight bot. "Why don't you find out where it's trying to go?"

Baymax picked up the petri dish. The bot continued to buzz in one specific direction. It was like a compass. Baymax followed it out of the room.

Moments later, horns honked and tires screeched. Baymax was outside!

Hiro needed to go after him. But he had to get past Aunt Cass.

"Hiro?" she said. She was happy to see him out of his room. "Are you registering for school?"

"Uh-huh," Hiro replied. He was afraid he'd get in trouble if he told her he was chasing a robot!

"Okay, special dinner tonight!" Aunt Cass said. She promised to make extra-hot chicken wings. But Hiro had already rushed outside to follow Baymax.

First, Baymax got on a trolley car. Hiro ran after him. Then Baymax went along some train tracks, and Hiro still couldn't catch him. When Baymax entered a mall, Hiro lost him in a crowd. He finally caught up with Baymax and the microbot at an old warehouse by the ocean.

Inside the warehouse, Hiro found barrels full of microbots. Someone must have stolen them! A giant machine was making even more!

Suddenly, the bots all came together and chased Baymax and Hiro! A man in a mask stood in the shadows, controlling the microbots.

"Run!" Hiro shouted to Baymax, who was moving slowly. "Go!"

Hiro pushed him and pulled him. The swarm got closer and closer. The microbots punched holes in Baymax.

Hiro and Baymax jumped out a window to escape. Luckily, Baymax cushioned Hiro's fall. They hurried to make a report at a police station.

The policeman Hiro spoke to didn't believe him. "All right. Let me get this straight. A man in a Kabuki mask attacked you with an army of miniature flying robots—"

"Microbots!" Hiro said. "Yeah, he was

controlling them telepathically with a neurocranial transmitter."

"Look, kid," the policeman said, reaching for his phone. "How about we call your parents?"

Hiro couldn't let him call home! Aunt Cass would be furious.

Hiro quickly grabbed Baymax and left. The police weren't going to help him. He had to catch the masked man alone.

Hiro needed to think.

Chapter 4

By the time they got home, Baymax was almost out of power. He was being difficult . . . and loud.

"Okay," Hiro whispered to Baymax. "If my aunt asks, we were at school all day. Got it?"

Baymax flopped onto the stairs. "We jumped out a window!" the robot shouted.

Hiro tried to quiet Baymax, but Aunt

Cass heard them go by.

"You home, sweetie?" she asked. She was cooking and had her back to Hiro. "Wings are almost ready!"

"Wings!" Baymax squealed. Aunt Cass turned to face Hiro. But she didn't see Baymax because Hiro had pushed him out of sight.

"Tell me everything!" she said.

"Uh, the thing is . . . ," Hiro said nervously. He needed to move Baymax upstairs. He didn't want to get in trouble! "Since I registered so late, I've got a lot to catch up on."

"Well, at least take a plate for the road!" Aunt Cass said, disappointed.

Hiro took the plate and pushed Baymax upstairs. He sighed when he had finally gotten Baymax to stand inside his charging station.

"This is crazy. It doesn't make any sense," Hiro said, sitting on his bed. He pulled out his microbot and stared at it. *Who was that guy in the mask?* he thought. *And how did he get my microbots?*

"Tadashi," Baymax said. The robot looked around the room. He saw Tadashi's baseball hat on his bed. "Tadashi," Baymax repeated.

"Tadashi's gone," Hiro said.

"When will he return?" Baymax asked.

"He's dead, Baymax."

Baymax pointed at his chest. "Tadashi is here—"

"I know," Hiro said, "people keep saying he's here; he's not really gone as long as we remember him. It still hurts."

But Baymax continued: "You are my patient. I would like to help."

"You can't fix this one, buddy," Hiro said.

Baymax went over to Hiro's computer. "I am downloading information on personal loss," the helpful bot reported. "Treatments include contact with friends and loved ones. I am contacting them now." The computer screen showed images of Wasabi, Go Go, Honey, and Fred.

Baymax gave Hiro a hug. "Other treatments include compassion and physical reassurance." He patted Hiro's back. "There, there."

Hiro smiled. "Thanks, Baymax," he said softly. He remembered Tadashi's hugs.

"I am sorry about the fire," Baymax said.

"It's okay. It was an accident."

Saying it made Hiro think of that terrible day. *Why didn't I stop Tadashi from going into that building?* he asked himself.

Then he realized something: "The guy in the mask! He set the fire so no one would know he had stolen my microbots!"

Hiro hurried down to his computer in the garage. He wanted to teach

Baymax some fighting moves—the ones his little fight bot had used to win. Hiro was ready to hunt down the masked man.

Baymax was curious. "Will apprehending the man in the mask improve your emotional state?"

"Absolutely."

Hiro created a full set of armor for Baymax using his 3-D printer. Then he downloaded karate moves onto a red computer chip. He opened Baymax's access panel. A green computer chip was already inside, with something written on it: **TADASHI HAMADA**.

Hiro stopped. *Tadashi,* he thought.

Is this what Tadashi would do?

Hiro put the red computer chip next to Tadashi's green one, then closed the

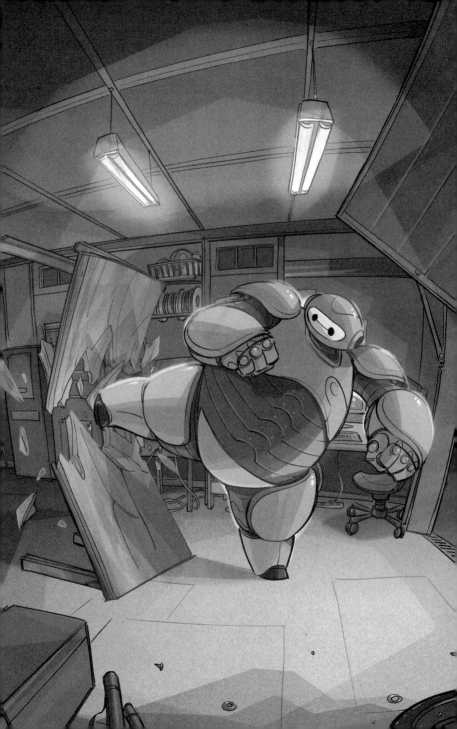

panel. Baymax began downloading the new data.

Baymax could now perform fighting moves. He was also protected by armor! Baymax practiced some karate.

"Side kick!" Hiro shouted. Baymax kicked a board in half. They were ready to face the masked man!

Chapter 5

That night, Baymax and Hiro returned to the old warehouse. It was empty.

Hiro looked at the microbot he'd brought with him. It began rattling so hard in its dish that the lid flew off. The microbot was free! It zipped through the air and disappeared in the fog over the ocean.

Moments later, a large swarm of microbots emerged from the fog. They carried a huge metal piece of some unknown machine—and the masked man! Hiro was scared. *What is this guy up to?*

The man rode on top of the swarm of microbots. The power and size of the microbots all working together was frightening.

Hiro and Baymax hid behind a large metal shipping container. The bright glow of headlights surprised Hiro. Then the light went out. Go Go, Honey, Wasabi, and Fred jumped out of a car! They had followed Hiro to the warehouse after Baymax had contacted them.

"No!" Hiro hissed. He waved at them to go away. He didn't want the masked man to see them. "Get out of here! Go!"

But it was too late. The man turned

and saw the group. He quickly made the microbots throw a giant shipping container at the friends!

Baymax moved in front of the box and stopped it from falling on the group. He saved them!

Go Go shoved Hiro into the car with Wasabi, Fred, and Honey. A group of microbots slammed into Baymax! They flung him through the air and he landed hard on the car's roof.

"Hiro. Explanation. Now," Go Go ordered as Wasabi drove as fast as he could.

Hiro told them about the man in the mask. "He stole my microbots. He started the fire!"

Suddenly, Wasabi braked.

"Why did we stop?" Go Go yelled.

Wasabi pointed at the traffic signal and started to explain, "The light's red!"

"There are no red lights in a car chase!" Go Go screamed.

Go Go pushed Wasabi out of the way and started driving. The car zipped along the streets at top speed.

The masked man had the microbots make a ramp in front of the car. Go Go raced to the top—and their car ran off the real road and into the ocean.

The man with the mask watched the car sink. Then he left, riding on a wave of microbots.

The car was now completely underwater. The friends tried to get out.

Baymax quickly took off his armor and grabbed all five of them. He filled

with air and floated everyone to the surface. Baymax had saved them again! As they got back on land, no one spoke about what would have happened if the robot hadn't been there.

Hiro looked around, still feeling a little scared. "We should get out of here."

"I know a place!" Fred said.

The cold, wet group walked through the streets. Fred said his house was close by. But it wasn't a house, it was a *mansion!*

"Welcome to *mi casa!*" Fred shouted. "That's French for 'front door'!" He grinned.

The door opened and a butler greeted Fred and his friends with a small bow.

"Welcome home, Master Frederick!"

Fred led his surprised friends through the big home to his bedroom. It was filled with posters from comic books and life-sized superhero suits.

Baymax gave everyone medical attention. They talked about what had happened.

"Does this symbol mean anything to you guys?" Hiro held up a picture he had drawn. It looked like a bird. Hiro had seen it on the big piece of machinery

the microbots were carrying. No one knew what it was.

"Apprehending the man in the mask will improve Hiro's emotional state," Baymax said.

Fred agreed. He also decided that the villain needed a name, so he called him Yokai, the Japanese word for "bad guy." Then he sat down at his computer. "I have a theory," he said. He pulled up the image of . . . Alistair Krei!

"Think about it," Fred explained. "Krei wanted your microbots, and you said no. Rules don't apply to a man like Krei. If he doesn't get what he wants, he just takes it."

Hiro didn't believe Krei was the thief. But he didn't have any idea how to find out who was.

Just then, Baymax started listing Yokai's stats: "His blood type is AB negative. Cholesterol levels elevated. Blood pressure one thirty—"

"Baymax, you scanned him?" Hiro asked. "I can use the data from your scan to find him!"

"This is a job for the police. We're nerds!" Wasabi protested.

Hiro shook his head. "I tried the police," he said. "Trust me, I'm on my own."

"No, you're not. We're with you!" Go Go said. If Yokai was responsible for Tadashi's death, then Hiro's friends wanted to find him, too, and bring him to justice.

"Tadashi was my brother," Hiro said. "This is my fight."

But his friends insisted.

"Those who suffer a loss require the support of friends and loved ones," Baymax told Hiro. "Perhaps they would benefit from some upgrades."

Baymax pointed at a poster of comic-book heroes on Fred's wall. They could be like the heroes in the poster. They could all fight Yokai together.

"Can you feel it?" Fred asked. "Our origin story begins!"

They were a team now.

Chapter 6

The six friends got to work. Hiro worked with all of their tech to make new super suits for everyone. When they were finished, they took the gear out into Fred's garden to practice.

Honey got a colorful purse with an amazing built-in chemistry kit. It was cute—and dangerous. "I love it! I love it!" she shouted.

Hiro pointed to Fred's butler,

Heathcliff. Heathcliff pulled a Kabuki mask over his face. Honey threw chem-balls at him. The chem-balls covered Heathcliff in goo.

Go Go was upgraded with discs that were like wheels for her hands and feet. "Whoa!" she shouted. She moved her arms and legs to keep her balance. Then she took off. She grabbed a hose and skated circles around Heathcliff. The hose wrapped around him, holding him in place.

Hiro presented Fred with a suit that looked like a Japanese monster known as a Kaiju. "Super-jump!" Fred shouted. The elastic suit bounced him high into the air. "And I breathe fire!" He jumped even higher, and a circle of grass surrounding Heathcliff caught on fire.

Wasabi got laser gloves. "Whoa!" he said. He practiced cutting the mansion's decorative pillars, which then fell harmlessly to the ground.

Baymax got new armor, powerful rocket fists, wings, and thrusters for his feet!

Hiro made a suit for himself, too. His armor had powerful magnets in the hands and knees so he could hang on to Baymax when they flew.

"Show 'em what you got, buddy," Hiro said to Baymax.

Baymax's rocket fist launched from his arm and punched through a wall, then immediately returned to its original position.

Everyone was impressed. "Rocket fist make Freddie so happy!" Fred said.

"Baymax, wings!" Hiro shouted.

Wings extended from Baymax's back. Hiro climbed onto the robot. The first time they tried to take off, they fell to the ground. Baymax really needed to practice flying. "Let's just take this slow," Hiro said as they rose into the air. But Baymax flew super fast—faster than Hiro had ever gone in his life.

"Up, up, up! Thrust!" Hiro screamed as they soared through the air. They were still unsteady, but Hiro loved it.

Baymax scanned Hiro when they stopped. "Your dopamine levels are rising."

"Which means what?" Hiro asked.

"Your treatment is working," Baymax replied. Hiro *was* feeling better. He was feeling great!

They flew back into the air. This time, they went faster and higher.

At the end of the day, the team was ready.

Hiro had also given Baymax a more powerful sensor. Baymax scanned the city and found Yokai. The masked man was just off the coast of San Fransokyo. Baymax flew the friends to Akuma

Island. It was dark and creepy.

"The patient is somewhere in that structure," Baymax said. He pointed at a steel door to the biggest building on the island.

Wasabi cut through the door with his laser gloves.

The team sneaked inside. "With little to no chance of survival, they enter the belly of the beast," Fred whispered dramatically. He was living his comic-book dream.

They found a control room with a bank of video screens on one wall. Hiro saw the familiar bird image on a monitor. It was just like the one he had seen on the metal piece the microbots had been carrying. *We must be close!* Hiro thought.

Hiro touched a computer key and a video turned on. It showed Krei making a presentation.

"I present Project Silent Sparrow," Krei announced. "Teleportation: the transport of matter instantaneously through space. Not science fiction anymore. Science fact!"

Krei turned to a girl sitting in the pilot's seat of a small pod. "Ready to go for a ride, Abigail?"

She gave him a thumbs-up.

Krei smiled. The technicians began their work. A large, circular portal filled with swirling energy opened. Then a technician pointed to a computer monitor. Krei stopped smiling. He seemed to be thinking that something wasn't quite right. Evidently, he decided to take the chance anyway.

The pod launched into the portal. *KA-BOOM!* The portal mechanism broke apart, but not before the pod had disappeared inside it!

"The pilot is gone!" one of the technicians shouted.

The group of friends watched in horror. Then the video ended.

"He's stealing his machine back!" Hiro said. He realized that the microbots gave Yokai the power to find and move the heavy metal parts that made up the portal. "And he's using my microbots to do it. Fred, you were right. It's Krei."

"Oh, no," Baymax said, turning his head.

Yokai was standing right behind them with a group of microbots!

Chapter 7

The six heroes jumped into action. "Get the mask!" Hiro shouted. He knew that Yokai was controlling the microbots with it.

They battled Yokai. But the microbots made Yokai strong. He lashed out at them with the swarm of bots.

Honey threw a chem-ball at Yokai. But it missed, making ice on the floor.

Go Go slipped on the ice as she raced toward Yokai and knocked Honey down. Wasabi knocked away the microbots in the air with his laser gloves, but then he realized the bots were holding his legs in place. The team kept getting in one another's way and was no closer to stopping Yokai. They needed to work together.

Finally, Baymax and Hiro flew close to Yokai. Baymax was pushed back by the microbots, but Hiro jumped forward and knocked Yokai's mask off.

"It's over, Krei!" Hiro shouted to the back of Yokai's head.

Yokai turned.

Yokai was not Krei. It was Professor Callaghan!

Hiro was stunned. "But . . . but the

explosion. You died."

"No," Callaghan replied. "Your microbots kept me safe."

"But—Tadashi . . . you just let him die?" Hiro's voice got louder. "He went in there to save you!"

"That was his mistake!" Callaghan yelled back.

Hiro was overcome with anger. He stared at the professor. Then he turned to Baymax. "Destroy him."

Baymax couldn't do it. "Hiro, this is not what—"

Hiro opened Baymax's panel. He pulled out Tadashi's green computer chip, removing the programming that directed him to help people. "Do it, Baymax. Destroy him," Hiro ordered.

Baymax lifted his rocket-blasting

fist and attacked Callaghan.

"Get the nurse chip back into Baymax, now!" Go Go shouted to the others.

Hiro's friends loved him. And they missed Tadashi. But they could not let him destroy Professor Callaghan. They had to stop Baymax! Fred, Wasabi, Honey, and Go Go kept trying to grab the robot, but Baymax pushed them away. Honey was finally able to jam the green chip back inside him.

Baymax stopped fighting, and Callaghan moved quickly. He put on his mask. The microbots pushed Callaghan and the last piece of the portal out a hole in the roof!

Hiro was angry with his friends. "How could you do that? I had him!"

"Hey, what you just did—we never

signed up for that," Wasabi told him.

Hiro couldn't believe that his friends had held him back. The professor was a bad man. "Baymax, find Callaghan."

"My enhanced scanner has been damaged," the robot reported.

"AH!" Hiro yelled. He jumped onto Baymax's back. "Fly!" he shouted. They flew away, leaving the rest of the team stranded on the island.

At home, Hiro went to his computer. He quickly fixed Baymax's super sensor. Baymax watched from his charging station.

"Your blood pressure is elevated," Baymax reported. "You appear to be distressed."

"I'm fine!" Hiro yelled. He stood up and touched the panel on Baymax's chest. The panel didn't open!

"Wha—?" Hiro was confused. He wanted to remove Baymax's green computer chip.

"Will terminating Callaghan improve your emotional state?" Baymax asked.

"Yes! No. . . . I don't know."

Baymax refused to open his panel. "Is this what Tadashi would have wanted?"

"It doesn't matter," Hiro said. "Tadashi is gone."

"Tadashi is here," Baymax stated.

"No! He's not here," Hiro said.

"Tadashi is here," Baymax said.

Suddenly, Hiro heard Tadashi's voice. Baymax was playing a video of Tadashi that was stored in his memory.

"This is Tadashi Hamada, and this is the first test of my robotics project."

But the test was a mess. Different clips showed Tadashi trying over and over.

Until finally Tadashi said, "Okay. Eighty-fourth test. What do you say, big guy?"

Tadashi reached forward and pressed a button. His face lit up with joy. "It works! HE WORKS! AH! Ah, yes! This is amazing!"

Tadashi spun in his chair. He pumped his fist in the air. "Wait till my brother sees you!"

Hiro stood still and watched. A moment passed. A tear ran down his cheek.

Tadashi had made a nurse bot. He wanted to heal people. He didn't want to hurt anyone.

"Tadashi had to help," Hiro whispered. He understood now.

Just then, Hiro noticed that his friends were in the room—Fred, Wasabi, Honey, and Go Go.

"Guys, I'm . . . I'm—" Hiro said.

Go Go hugged Hiro. "We're going to catch Callaghan," she said.

"But maybe don't leave your team stranded on a spooky island next time?"

Wasabi said, and Go Go nodded.

Hiro felt awful. "Oh, man."

"It's cool." Fred smiled. "Heathcliff picked us up in the family chopper."

Honey held up a video chip from the island. "We found something you should see."

The friends gathered around Hiro's computer. They watched the first section of the video, which showed what had taken place before Krei's teleportation demonstration. Krei, Callaghan, and Abigail were all together.

Hiro looked closely at Abigail. He saw CALLAGHAN on her helmet. "The pilot was Callaghan's daughter. Callaghan blames Krei."

Fred stared at the video. "This is a revenge story."

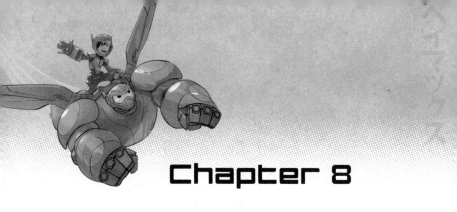

Chapter 8

Everything made sense now. Callaghan was the enemy. He had caused the fire at San Fransokyo Tech. He had stolen Hiro's microbots and created more. He had used the neural transmitter fitted into his Kabuki mask to control them. Callaghan had used the microbots to move pieces of the portal from Krei's lab on the island.

Hiro guessed that Callaghan was

headed to the grand opening of the new Krei Tech campus in San Fransokyo.

Meanwhile, Callaghan confronted Alistair Krei at the campus.

"You took everything from me when you sent Abigail into that machine!" Callaghan shouted.

Krei couldn't believe it. Callaghan was using the microbots to put the pieces of the portal back together. He wanted Krei to watch as he turned on the faulty portal. Once it was on, it would suck everything Krei had worked for inside and destroy it. Then he would send Krei into the portal, too.

The team got there just as Callaghan sent his microbots to capture Krei.

"Professor Callaghan!" Hiro yelled. "Let him go! Is this what Abigail would have wanted?" He knew how the professor felt. "This won't change anything. Trust me, I know."

Callaghan didn't listen. He wanted to destroy Krei!

The team jumped into action.

"Go for the mask!" Hiro yelled.

The team used all their powers, but they were losing.

"Listen up. Use those big brains of yours to think your way out. There are no dead ends!" Hiro told his friends.

He wanted them to work together. As a team, they were stronger than Callaghan and the microbots.

He told Fred to create smoke so they could hide from Callaghan, who

was at the top of a tower of microbots. Wasabi slashed the microbots with his laser gloves, keeping the swarm unfocused. Go Go threw her discs to make cracks in the tower of bots that held up Callaghan. Honey threw a chem-ball to deepen the cracks that Go Go had created. Together they knocked Callaghan to the ground and saved Krei from his enemy.

"No!" Callaghan cried.

Hiro directed Fred to grab the professor's mask. When it was taken from his face, the microbots fell to the ground. Because they had been holding the portal, the portal fell to the ground as well.

But it was still sucking everything inside! Baymax stared at the portal.

"We need to get out of here, now!" Hiro said, starting to worry. "Baymax!"

Baymax pointed toward the portal. "My sensor is detecting signs of life."

"Callaghan's daughter!" said Hiro. "She's still alive!" He looked at Baymax, and the two friends went into the portal together. They reached the pod. Abigail was alive but very weak. Hiro and Baymax had to save her!

Baymax turned on his thrusters and flew toward the portal exit. Hiro led him around the flying trash. *BAM!* Trash smashed into Baymax. His thrusters were broken. They would not be able to leave the portal.

"There is still a way I can get you both to safety," Baymax told Hiro. Baymax could save Hiro and Abigail, but not himself.

Hiro stared at his giant robot friend. Baymax would do anything to save him.

"What about you?" Hiro asked. "I need you."

He loved Baymax.

Baymax spoke softly. "I cannot deactivate until you say you are satisfied with your care."

Hiro's eyes filled with tears. To save Abigail, he would have to leave Baymax. Hiro hugged his friend.

"I am satisfied with my care," he said, starting to cry. Then he let go of Baymax. Forever.

Hiro used the magnets in his suit to attach himself to Abigail's pod. He felt a bump when Baymax's rocket glove hit it and blasted Hiro and

Abigail safely out of the portal.

Hiro cried as Baymax disappeared behind him.

Back at home, Hiro spent more time with Aunt Cass and his friends. But he never forgot Tadashi or Baymax.

He started college. With his friends by his side, Hiro enjoyed SFIT.

Then one day, Hiro glanced at Baymax's rocket glove. It was the only thing he had left of the robot.

He fist-bumped the hand, and the fingers opened. Hiro found a green object: Baymax's nurse chip! He grinned from ear to ear.

It didn't take long for Hiro to

make a new Baymax from that green computer chip. After all, he was Tadashi Hamada's little brother! Hiro turned the robot on.

"Hello, Hiro," Baymax said. "I am Baymax, your personal health-care companion."

Hiro smiled and threw his arms around his best friend.